For Emily and Henry.

Thanks to Kelvinside Kindergarten for their artistic hamster drawings
and Colours Model Agency for supplying the children.

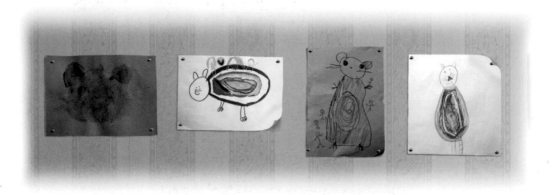

First published in Great Britain in 2014
by Piccadilly Press, a Templar/Bonnier publishing company
Deepdene Lodge, Deepdene Avenue, Dorking, Surrey RH5 4AT
www.piccadillypress.co.uk

Text and illustrations copyright © Lorna Freytag, 2014

Designed by Simon Davis
Printed and bound in China by WKT

ISBN: 978 1 84812 380 9 (h/b)
ISBN: 978 1 84812 379 3 (p/b)

1 3 5 7 9 10 8 6 4 2

My Humongous Hamster goes to School

LORNA FREYTAG

Piccadilly

Today is
'bring your pet to school' day.

So I bring my hamster.

Freddy brings his fish.
Maisie brings her rabbit.

My hamster has never
been to school before.

But my hamster gets out of his cage –
he must be hungry!

He eats my packed lunch.
He eats EVERYONE'S packed lunch.

And then my hamster begins to

GROW

and

GROW . . .

Everyone starts looking
at him and laughing.
The teacher tells my hamster
to sit down and behave.

But my humongous hamster
breaks the chair.

The teacher
is not pleased.

When the bell goes,
the girls start their
music and dance class.

My humongous hamster
tries to join in,
but keeps getting
in their way!

Afterwards the teacher suggests
we settle down and do some painting.

I draw my hamster.
EVERYONE draws my hamster.

We ask my humongous hamster
which one he likes best.

But he just EATS the paintings . . .

. . . and that's when things
get **worse**!

Our teacher goes to find the head teacher,
but my hamster follows her.

He peers into all the classrooms.

He upsets the dinner ladies
in the school canteen

and eats all the dinners.

He climbs on all the gym equipment.

'Get down,' I tell him.
'Get down now!'

But he doesn't get down for ages.

He goes outside
into the
playground.

He likes to
play hopscotch.

He is too big
for the slide,

but he loves
the roundabout!

But then the head teacher tells him off for being so naughty and sends him to sit in the corner.

He sits there quietly.

So I give him a hug.

Then the whole class gives him a hug.

After that, bit by bit,

my hamster shrinks back

to normal hamster size.

Then it's time to go home.

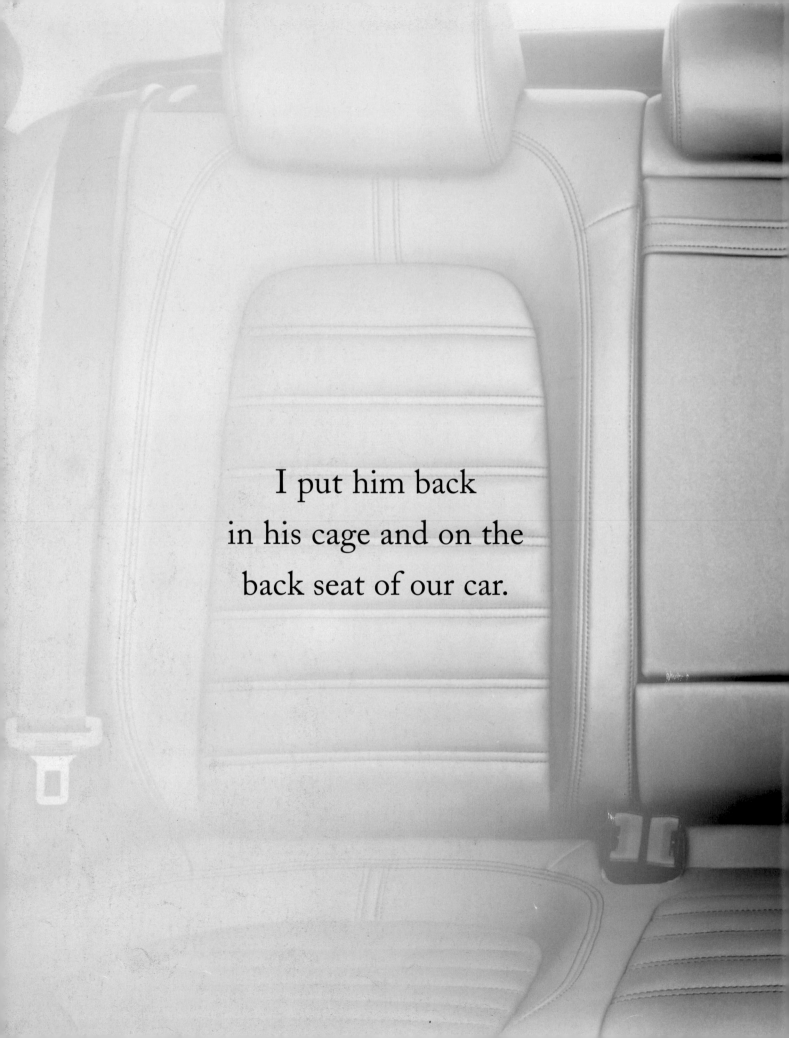

I put him back
in his cage and on the
back seat of our car.

My mum asks
if I've had a nice day.

But I just say,
'Nah, it was boring.'

Well, I don't want to
get my hamster in trouble . . .

. . . do I?